Jean M. Aka. e daughter of a librarian and was introduced to books at an early age. She could read by the time she started school and thinks, even in this technological age, books are still important in the development of children's imaginations.

Jean feels many bullied children lead a solitary life, but can lose themselves and feel they need not be alone when they read positive, supportive books like *Simon and the Little Green Man*. They find in the story that bullying can be overcome even if they never meet their own little green alien friend.

Simon and the Little Green Man is Jean's second published children's story.

D1136534
301302

Simon and the Little Green Man

Also by Jean M. Akam

The Virtual Reality Space Pirates

Jean M. Akam

Simon and the Little Green Man

Nightingale Books

NIGHTINGALE PAPERBACK

© Copyright 2018
Jean M. Akam
Illustrated by Doug Smith

The right of Jean M. Akam to be identified as author of
this work has been asserted by her in accordance with the
Copyright, Designs and Patents Act 1988.

All Rights Reserved

No reproduction, copy or transmission of this publication
may be made without written permission.
No paragraph of this publication may be reproduced,
copied or transmitted save with the written permission of the
publisher, or in accordance with the provisions
of the Copyright Act 1956 (as amended).

Any person who commits any unauthorised act in relation to
this publication may be liable to criminal
prosecution and civil claims for damages.

A CIP catalogue record for this title is
available from the British Library.

ISBN 978 1 912021 88 8

Nightingale Books is an imprint of
Pegasus Elliot MacKenzie Publishers Ltd.
www.pegasuspublishers.com

First Published in 2018

Nightingale Books
Sheraton House Castle Park
Cambridge England

Printed & Bound in Great Britain

Dedication

To Gemma, Jake and Molly Brown my
inspirational grandchildren and Rory
Dunbar.

Acknowledgements

Thanks to Doug Smith for his amazing, inspirational illustrations which brought *Simon and the Little Green Man* alive.

To the staff at Pegasus for their continuing support.

Also, to my supportive family and friends for their continuing interest in my writing.

Simon stared at his computer screen in disbelief. He had just zapped the little green man from Mars with his space blaster and not only had the little green man disappeared, so had the whole game. He frantically pressed a few keys and moved his mouse about, but to no avail - nothing re-appeared. He felt extremely puzzled, then all was revealed when he heard a loud giggle and a "Simey Whiney, looking for this?"

Turning around, he saw his sister, Sarah. She was standing in the doorway of his bedroom with a plug in her hand. She started to swing it about, taunting him.

Suddenly, to Simon's horror, the face of Mark Baxter, the school bully, appeared around the door. "Oh Simon, I believe you know my new boyfriend," said his sister.

'This is the end,' thought Simon. Not only did he have to stand the bullying from Mark Baxter in the school playground, he was now united with his sister against him. If he really was her boyfriend and it was not just a ghastly joke, then Simon wouldn't even have a bolthole at home.

For years, Simon had had to put up with his sister mocking him, pinching him and telling tales to their parents. If she broke anything, Simon always got the blame. Sometimes, if she was feeling very spiteful, she used to cry for no reason other than getting Simon punished.

'Girls,' thought Simon, 'are a pain.' His sister could turn the tears on at the drop of a hat. Every time this happened, Simon's father used to ask him what pleasure he got out of bullying his sister and then banned him from playing computer games for a day or two.

'It just isn't fair,' thought Simon. If only he could stand up to his sister. Problem was, she was ten and a half and quite a bit taller than he was. Even though he wasn't much younger than Sarah, nine to be precise, he was small for his age, with ginger hair and freckles, and had to wear glasses for reading and playing computer games.

His sister had started off calling him "Owley, Wowley" and then the usual "Four Eyes" people who wore glasses often got called. When he was younger, he had cried when she teased and bullied him and her mocking, "Simey, Whimey is a cry baby," turned into "Simey Whiney" and had stuck ever since. Now everyone called him that. Even his mother had called him it once. It was all too much.

"Dad wants you," said Sarah. "He seems to think you have a use."

Simon sighed. Not only had Sarah wiped his score off the screen, he couldn't remember it. The only thing he could remember was two more Martian space ships and he would have saved the world from the Martian invasion. He would have been a hero. Trouble is, when you are small in size and bullied by everyone, you have to be able to feel brave now and again.

'If only I could do this in real life,' thought Simon, 'life would be so different.'

His sister and Mark were laughing as they left the room. As if this was not enough, as a final act, Mark had stuffed some chewing gum in the socket that his computer was plugged into. Simon sighed and removed the gum. It stuck to everything. Just as he was pulling the last bit off, his mother appeared.

"Oh Simon," she said, "why do you have to be so naughty? Why can't you be more like Mark, he's such a nice boy?"

Simon was speechless. How could she say that? Looking past his mother, he saw the leering faces of Sarah and Mark. Sarah stuck her tongue out at him and Mark pulled a face. Simon's mother turned around and Sarah and Mark's faces resumed a more normal expression.

"Come on Simon", said his mother, "your father is waiting". She went downstairs. As Simon passed Mark a foot suddenly shot out and tripped him up. He stumbled and his mother turned around.

"Why are you so clumsy, Simon?" she sighed.

Simon felt tears pricking his eyelids. He sniffed and Sarah whispered yet again, "Simey Whiney, cry baby."

At that moment, Simon hated the World.

Simon went downstairs and met his father waiting impatiently in the hallway. "Aren't you ready yet?" he said.

Simon put on his jacket and followed his father out to the car. His father was tiling the bathroom and needed to buy some more tiles and paint. He was always saying that Simon did not get enough fresh air and he had decided that a trip out would be good for him.

'Why does no one ever ask me what I want to do?' thought Simon, feeling most hard done by. His sister never got dragged away from what she enjoyed doing, so why should he? Why did he have to be different all the time?

After what seemed like an eternity when they got stuck in a traffic jam, they finally pulled into the car park of the Cheapo D.I.Y. store. His father strode off to the entrance of the store. This meant Simon had to run after him. He felt very out of breath and cross.

His father wandered around the shelves. Then he suddenly said to a person's back, "Hi Joe, fancy meeting you here."

Joe turned around. He worked with Simon's father. They started talking. After what seemed like an age Simon looked at his watch. His father had been talking to Joe for fifteen minutes. Simon wondered how they could have so much to say to each other. After all, they saw each other every day at work.

After a while his father noticed that Simon was looking rather bored so he said to him, "Here's some money. Go to the food bar in here and I'll meet you there when I've finished talking to Joe."

Simon looked around him. The store was a huge place and whilst his father had been talking to Joe, they had wandered up and down the aisles. Simon hadn't got the slightest idea where the food bar was and his father had now disappeared. Being so short, Simon immediately had a problem. He looked up and along the shelving; there seemed to be miles and miles of it stretching in all directions.

Simon could imagine how people felt when they got lost in mazes. The highly stacked shelves suddenly seemed to close in on him ominously and he felt that he was shrinking. Suddenly, a metal nut flew past his head and clunked neatly into a toolbox on the floor.

It was a good thing that Simon had seen the nut, otherwise he would have tripped over the toolbox which was directly in his path. The box was bright green in colour and glowed. It was round in shape with black, unreadable squiggles around its edge. The hinged lid was open and another metal nut dropped into the box next to the first one in a very controlled fashion. It made no noise when it landed and it seemed to be directed into a set space in the box. It was followed by yet another nut and then an assortment of screws and tools. Simon watched this procession of assorted metal objects with fascination. He turned to find out where they were coming from. They seemed to be flying off different shelves in a very co-ordinated way.

Suddenly, from behind a stack of wood propped up against a shelf, appeared a little green man. Simon stared in disbelief.

The man was the stuff of people's nightmares or imagination if you were a believer in alien visits. He was about half a metre tall, give or take the odd centimetre, and wore a tight-fitting suit that toned with the colour of his pea green face. The only other colour was the dark green of his belt. This had a rectangular box shape on it where a buckle should have been. It had buttons on it and glowed eerily. His hands had three, very long, boney like fingers on each one and in his left hand was a triangular shaped instrument. The green man pointed it at the shelves and it emitted a humming sound.

Simon suddenly panicked. It was all very well being heroic on a computer screen - after all, the alien creatures there couldn't really zap you into oblivion or kidnap you and take you into their space ships.

'What a position to be in,' thought Simon. His knees started to feel like jelly and he had a sick feeling in his stomach. He hurriedly looked over his shoulder.

Whichever way he ran, he would never get to the end of the shelving and around the corner before the little green man zapped him. Perhaps he should beg for mercy or say "take me to your leader" in a heroic fashion. He decided to brazen it out. Taking a deep breath, he stared straight into the green man's long, thin eyes.

They both looked each other up and down. Simon noticed the green man's small, pointed ears, thin nose with three holes in the end of it and his small, slit-like mouth. All Simon could think about was: 'It's true, there are little green men out there.'

All of a sudden, the little green man's nose wrinkled up and his mouth went up at the corners.

'Is he smiling at me or what?' thought Simon. He decided to take a chance and tentatively smiled back. The man removed the rectangular box from his belt and handed it to Simon after pressing a button that raised a small, computer like screen.

Simon backed away, but the green man continued to apparently smile and he thrust the box at Simon. He gestured at a button on the box with the middle finger of the three on his left hand. Simon, after a moment's hesitation, pressed the button and waited for something to happen.

'At least it hasn't exploded,' he thought.

The box made an electronic like noise and then the word 'English' appeared on the little screen attached to the box. The little green man then started to speak to Simon. He explained that the box understood which language Simon spoke from his finger print pattern on the button he had pressed.

He went on to tell Simon that his name was Tark and he was from Mars.

"Far out," shouted Simon. His voice echoed along the shelving.

A man and a woman appeared and the man said to him, "Are you OK, son?" The man was standing dangerously close to Tark. Simon realised that the man was showing no surprise at being confronted by a Martian. He was just about to tell the man to mind the toolbox on the floor when he noticed that Tark had used his space tool to elevate it. The round, green box's lid closed and it moved in a slow, deliberate motion onto an empty shelf.

This happened under the man's nose and still he showed no concern. Simon noticed that Tark's smile had turned into more of a smirk as he noticed Simon's bewilderment. Simon suddenly realised that neither the man nor the woman could see Tark or his toolbox.

"Yes, I'm OK, thanks," said Simon to the man and he and the woman moved on along the shelves.

"Are you really invisible?" said Simon to Tark.

Tark smiled and said, "Adults grow out of lots of things. Most of them just do not believe in little green men and once you stop believing in something, you can no longer see it even when it's right under your nose."

"That's really sad," said Simon.

"Yes, isn't it?" said Tark, agreeing with Simon. "I really would like to talk to your adults to let them know that we people from Mars mean them no harm."

Simon then questioned Tark as to what he was doing in a D.I.Y. store so far away from home. Tark told him that he was part of an expeditionary fleet, which was studying certain planets to see if their inhabitants could be approached in order to visit them and exchange information. Unfortunately, Tark had never been very good at the hovering manoeuvre. He was wonderful at flying fast both the right way up and upside down and boomeranging backwards and forwards around asteroids and chunks of space debris, but when it came to slowing down, he had problems. The thing was he liked speed - travelling at the speed of light was his idea of really living. When he was being taught to fly his space vehicle, he had not taken too much notice of his flying instructor when he was teaching the slowing down, hovering and stopping techniques. In fact, Tark had failed his flying test three times and only just managed to pass on his fourth attempt. His examiner had been distracted by a meteor, which had suddenly flashed across the sky. By the time he had recovered, Tark had had time to collect his thoughts and had pressed the right button. He had executed a really smooth stopping manoeuvre and his examiner had been very impressed.

The examiner had then approached a space official he knew and Tark was offered a posting on the Martian Space Exploration ship, 'The Nova Terrax'. This was a great honour as each ship was flown single handedly and so were only given to competent navigators. Everything had gone smoothly until Tark programmed the ship to hover over what turned out to be Simon's school. He had done no hovering at all in space and he realised that he had forgotten which button to press on the bank of buttons that controlled the ship. He scratched his head and went to find his space manual that he had put in a safe place. It was so safe, he couldn't remember where it was.

Tark had never been organised. His mother often despaired at his untidiness. He started to pull up the hatches on the container pods on the ship. He started to throw out tools, spare space suits, space boots, gloves and bits of smelly space munch, or food to those not familiar with Martian eating habits. The munch had started growing red things on its squelchy blue surface. These small,

Red Space Buglets tramped up and down through the goo that had once been Tark's space rations.

"Good grief," thought Tark, "where did they come from?" They hadn't been there when he left Mars. However, the Martian Red Space Buglet was well known for its deviousness and the colony had probably smuggled itself on board prior to take off. He picked up a disposal pod and shovelled the space food, Buglets and all, into it. Putting the disposal pod in the disposal hatch, he jettisoned it into space. As Martians believe that space is important and should not be cluttered with debris, as it is both dangerous and unhealthy, he zapped it with the ship's disintegrator weapon and it disappeared from sight.

As the 'Nova Terrax' was travelling very fast, Tark was horrified to find he was approaching Earth too fast. Suddenly, he remembered which button he should press to slow his vessel down for hovering. He pressed it and the 'Nova Terrax' slowed down, but it was not quick enough.

The ship plummeted into a tree on the edge of the school playground and was stuck in the branches.

When Tark had recovered from the shock of his crash landing, he estimated the damage to the ship. He needed quite a lot of repair type equipment or he would never be able to repair the ship and would then be stranded on Earth forever. He switched on his ship's invisibility screen and went to explore outside. He sat in the branches and measured how far down to the ground it was with his space measure. Pressing another button, a glowing pathway appeared from the end of the branch to the ground. Tark slid down it. Waiting only long enough to retract the pathway, he surveyed the land around him. Simon's school was on the outskirts of the town and the Cheapo D.I.Y. store had been built on land across the road from the school.

Using the box on his belt, Tark translated Cheapo and D.I.Y. into Martian.

'Just the place I want,' he thought to himself. He pressed another button on the box to work out the co-ordinates of the school and the D.I.Y. store and used its teleporting facility to beam himself across to the store. He had been sorting out what he needed when he met Simon.

Simon said he would help Tark to mend his ship. Tark pressed the button and Simon found himself the same size as Tark and inside the space ship. Tark took him on a guided tour which pleased Simon no end. At long last he had a friend and someone who took him seriously. They worked together, Simon holding the toolbox and passing Tark the tools and parts he wanted. Whilst he was helping Tark, Simon told him about his sister and the school bully.

"Don't worry," said Tark, "I'll sort them out for you".

The space ship took off and Simon guided Tark to his house. He took Tark up to his bedroom after Tark made him into normal size again by pressing another button on his buckle box. Simon offered to show Tark his computer games and decided not to show him the one in which you had to zap Martians.

In the middle of playing an adventure game in the jungle that had taken Tark's fancy as he had never seen a jungle, Simon's sister appeared with Mark.

Sarah was just about to have a go at Simon when she noticed Tark. She screamed, "What's that?"

Mark became very quiet and started to run away. Simon stared in amazement. 'Now who is the coward,' he thought.

Tark transferred himself with the help of his buckle box to the hallway just as Mark reached the bottom step.

"Let me out," shrieked Mark.

"Not until you and Sarah promise me you will leave Simon alone," said Tark.

"OK, OK, we will", they shouted.

"If you don't," said Tark, "I will come back and sort you out. After all I can become invisible and you will never know when I am watching you." Tark then went back to Simon's room to say goodbye.

"Can you take me back to the food bar at the store?" said Simon. "Otherwise Dad will be looking for me,"

"Sure thing", said Tark. "Thanks for everything".

"Thank you too", said Simon, "for sorting out Sarah and Mark."

"Don't mention it," said Tark, smiling at him. "If ever you need me again, just put this disc in your computer. It will send me a message and I will come back." He then pressed the buttons on his buckle box and they both disappeared

Simon found himself on his own at the entrance to the food bar. He waited for his father to meet him.

The following week, Sarah and Mark treated Simon with respect. However, old habits die hard and they started teasing him again in the playground. A crowd of their friends gathered and Mark began to tease Simon about Tark.

"Go on, Simey Whiney, tell them about your little green friend", he said.

"What little green friend?" said Simon. He was no longer afraid of either Mark or Sarah. He had seen how they had behaved when confronted by Tark. Sarah became annoyed. She had never seen her Brother like this. He wasn't playing her game.

"But we saw your little green man. Don't play the innocent with me. Mark and I saw him."

Their friends started to laugh at her and Mark.

Mark was furious, he wasn't used to people laughing at him. Their friends started to drift away, still laughing. Sarah started to cry and went up to

Mark. He told her to go away, he wasn't her boyfriend any more.

"Now you know how I have felt", said Simon to his sister. "It's not nice is it?"

"No", said Sarah. "I'm sorry I have been so horrible to you."

She and Mark were never horrible to Simon again.